The Ending of the Path:
A Collection of Haiku

Brett C. Persson

The Ending of the Path:

A Collection of Haiku

All Rights Reserved

Copyright © 2023 by Brett C. Persson

𝕏

@BrettCPersson

www.brettcpersson.com

Nudous Publishing, LLC

www.nudouspublishing.com
info@nudouspublishing.com

Paperback ISBN: 978-1-964793-88-7

Dedication

This is my last poetry book, and I dedicate it to my family and friends that have been my rock through good times and bad. I could not have asked for a more loving and supportive group of people in my life. They have been there for me during my years of addiction and never held it against me. In my recovery, they supported me. They have always believed in me, even when I didn't believe in myself, and for that, I am eternally grateful. This book is for them, with all my love.

Thank you for everything.

Table of Contents

Nature

Pedal Of Rose Falls

Ripples The Still Cold Water

Soon Calm Has Returned

Frog On Lily Pad

Dragonfly Hovers In Air

Mallard Softly Swims

Lightning Strikes The Ground

Orange Flames Lick The Night Sky

Nature's Housekeeping

Cold Breeze From The North

Daylight Slumbering Longer

Approaching Winter

The Sun Through The Trees

Leaves Turning In The Cool Air

Fall Has Come Early

Still Across The Pond

A Rock Enters The Water

Suddenly Alive

Water Ebbs and Flows

Tide Going Out As Sun Sets

Quiet On The Beach

Two Swans On The Lake

Gliding Gracefully Around

Elegant Beauty

Soft Petals Of Spring

A Whisper Of Fragrant Blooms.

Beauty Of Nature

Birds Sing In The Sun

Babbling Creeks Flow Through The Woods

The Rustle Of Trees

Crickets Chirp At Dusk

Serene Lakes Reflecting Stars

Nature's Harmony

Birds In Flight Soar High

Gliding Through The Azure Sky

Elegance In Flight

Pond Reflects The Sun

Dancing Willows In A Breeze

Tranquility Found

Butterflies Flutter

Dragonflies Circle Around

Enjoying The Day

Song Of Nightingale

Chirping Of Sparrows So Sweet

Nature's Choir Sings Loud

Trees Full Of Green Life

Flowers Bloom In Vivid Hues

A Wondrous Beauty

Going For A Walk

Through Lush And Vibrant Gardens

Free From Life's Worries

Little Twig Snapping

Rustling Leaves As They Run By

Kids Running Around

Rolling Hills, So Vast

The Land Lush Green Foliage

Astounding Beauty

Water Over Rocks

Cascading Of Waterfalls

A Majestic Scene

Birds Singing Sweetly

A Natural Paradise

Rainbows In The Sky

Reflections Look Back

Sun Sets Over The Still Lake

Beauty Of The Sun

Glowing Orange Sun

Horizon Captured In Time

View Of Sun Setting

Peaceful Serenade

Squirrels Scamper And Frolic

Laughing In Delight

The Night Sky Twinkles

Countless Stars Like Diamond Dust

Wonder Breathlessly

Victoria Falls

The World's Largest Waterfall

The Smoke That Thunders

The Great Grand Canyon

Expanse Of Desert Beauty

Awe-Inspiring Sight

Astonishing Sights

Yellowstone National Park

Nature At Its Best

Up In The Night Sky

Vast Expanse Of Stars Twinkle

Out In The Darkness

The Void Between Us

Cosmic Dust And Starlight Swirls

Making Galaxies

Salty Air And Mist

Waves Crashing On The Shoreline

Mystic Songs On Wind

Seabirds Fly Above

Sharks In Murky Depths Below

Enchanting Creatures

Ocean Calls Us Forth

Inviting Us To Explore

Mysterious Realm

Endless Rolling Tides

Sea Of Blue That Changes Moods

Ocean Vast And Wide

Coral In Shallows

Life Abounding In The Depths

Nothing Can Compare

Soaring Gracefully

The Wings Of A Butterfly

A Master In Flight

Artists Vibrant Hues

Kaleidoscope Of Beauty

Gentle Creature Glides

The Stream Flows Calmly

Fish Swimming Along The Edge

Salmon Traveling

The Green Blades Of Grass

Fragrant And Sweet Aroma

Glistening In Dew

Peaceful And Serene

Cabin Nestled In The Woods

Far Away From Town

Wind Whistling Through Trees

Moss-Covered Logs And Rafters

The Smell Of Pine Bark

Birdsong Rings Throughout

Blanket Of Golden Leaves Fall

Solitude Found Here

Crickets Play In Tune

Stillness That Is Comforting

Nature's Orchestra

Evergreens Swaying

Distant Snowy Mountain Range

A Peaceful Retreat

Deep In Murky Swamp

A Chorus Of Frogs Singing

Mosquitoes Abound

A Dim Mist Hangs Low

Crocodiles Skulk In Shadows

Birds Sitting On Trees

Trees With Spanish Moss

Stalks Of Cattails Rustling Soft

The Damp Soil Squishing

Toads Croak From Mud Banks

Dragonflies Skim Across Pads

Gators Hunt Nearby

The Sun Sets Slowly

Night Creatures Come Out To Play

Peacefulness Descends

Deserts Vast And Dry

Sun Blazes Bright In The Sky

Life Teeming Below

Oasis Of Life

Cool Water Offers Relief

A Watering Hole

Cacti Standing Tall

The Rugged Wasteland Terrain

Harsh But Beautiful

Sandy Dunes Shifting

Vastness Seems Without An End

Horizon So Grand

Wildlife Roams Freely

Tumbling Tumbleweed Around

The Desert's Embrace

The Snow Swirls And Spins

A blizzard Engulfs The Land

White Wind Whips Harshly

Freezing Gusts Of Air

Chaos Of Snowflakes Dancing

Frost Covered Branches

Gray Sky Hides The Sun

Icicles Hang Down Like Swords

Silent Winter Chill

Lonely Howling Winds

Snow Drifts Pile Up High Quickly

An Eerie Stillness

The Gentle Rain Falls

Cool Mist In The Morning Air

Kissing The Tree's Leaves

The Sky Hangs Heavy

Droplets Of Moisture Collect

Dancing On Way Down

Gently Starts To Pour

Filling Up Both Soil And Streams

Bringing life With It

Religion

Burden Of The Cross

Carried It Without Question

Sacrificed For Us

The Man Kneels Broken

He Raises His Hands Upward

God Heals His Hurt Soul

All Of Human Kind

We Aspire To Be Happy

And Not To Suffer

Praise Be To Allah

Submit To The Will Of God

Kaaba In Mecca

Walking The Lord's Path

The Teachings Of Jesus Christ

Path To Salvation

Respecting Them All

Open Heart And Open Mind

The Path Of Others

Cup Of Salvation

The Blood And Body Of Christ

Redeemed For Our Sins

Timeless Faith Of Man

Mysteries Beyond Our Grasp

A Hope That Shines Bright

Where Ancient Scrolls Lay

Ponderings Of Old Wise Souls

Insight They Impart

Unseen Angels Soar

Whispering Of Divine Will

Grace Lives In The World

Prophets Speak Their Truth

Faith's Power Woven In Us

How We Live Our Lives

Ancient Gods Of Old

Grew Out Of The Stars And Sky

A Religion Formed

From Ages Long Past

Worshipped Deities Divine

Passing Traditions

Rituals And Prayers

Between Our Cultures And Faiths

All Striving For Peace

A Symbol Of Grace

Devotion To Our Savior

Forgiveness For Souls

Christianity

Light Of Our Holy Savior

Spreading His Grace Far

A Beacon Of Faith

Refuge For The Faithful Few

God's Esteemed Children

Through Prayer And Fasting

To Be Humble In His Sight

Lives Forever Changed

We Look Up With Joy

Knowing He Is Always Near

Our Guide Through The Storm

Believe Fervently

Word Of The Lord Is Divine

Following With Faith

The Ultimate Goal

Soul's Redemption From Sin's Toll

Peace Through Salvation

God Is Their Refuge

Follow Closely His Teachings

Guidance For Their Paths

His Grace And Mercy

To Those Who Seek Him With Heart

Trust In His Promise

Path Of Salvation

Leading To A Life Of Grace

His Love Is Our Guide

The Almighty God

His Message Of Hope And Love

Life Is His Design

Moses Was Chosen

Creed Of Faith And Tradition

Preserved Through The Years

Teachings Of The Wise

Holy People, The Chosen

God's Faithful Servants

Holy Book Of God

Laws Of Moses Given Down

From The Lord On High

Buddhist Path Of Peace

Leads To Life Of Contentment

Living Harmony

The Wisdom Teachings

Passed Down Through Generations

Leading Thoughtful Lives

On Journey Ahead

We Strive To Follow The Way

Be Kind And Gentle

Let Go Attachments

No Need Material Greed

Seeking Inner Joy

Enlightenment Found

When Focused On Compassion

Achieve Inner Peace

Buddha Of The East

Your Teachings Bring A Great Peace

Eyes Closed, Stillness Found

Enlightenment Path

Exploration Of The Self

Meditation Truths

Clarity Within

Insightful Words And Knowledge

Harmony Attained

Noble Eightfold Path

Right View, Thought, Speech And Action

Way To Inner Peace

Grace Of Compassion

A Life Without Suffering

Freedom Found Within

Addiction & Recovery

The Numbing Of Pain

Drug Addiction Consumes Life

An Endless Spiral

A Helpless Abyss

Deceivingly Alluring

Life Slowly Erodes

Escaping The Grasp

Of This Insidious Curse

Seems Impossible

Desperate And Scared

Fighting The Growing Cravings

Despair In Darkness

Alone In The Night

Life Numbed By Substances Found

No End To Be Seen

Crying Solitude

Head Spinning With Addiction

Lost In A Spiral

Substances Beckon

Tempting The Mind And Body

Life Slowly Dwindling

Gripped By These Cravings

Yearning For Its Empty Bliss

Hope Ever Fleeting

Fog Of Despair Looms

An Endless Cycle Of Pain

Torment Unending

Shadows Take Over

Struggling Against The Cravings

Crushing Oppression

A Way Out Desired

Buried By False Promises

Despair Never Ends

My Life Numbed By Drugs

Desperate, Scared, And Alone

Gripped By Addiction

An Endless Cycle

Substances Offer False Bliss

Life Erodes Slowly

Shadows Of The Mind

Dazed With Insatiable Want

Life In The Crosshairs

Innocent Dreams Dashed

Fading Away Without Thought

Motivation Lost

Deadly Alluring

No End In Sight As Days Pass

A Slow Quiet Death

Cravings Consume Life

Deep-rooted Spiral Of Pain

Searching For Release

Pulling My Soul Down

An Insurmountable Force

A Sentence Of Death

Fear Rising Within

My Soul Is Catatonic

Lost In Confusion

Screaming In My Mind

Cries In The Still Of The Night

Hope Slowly Dying

Life Cloaked By Sadness

Soul Shaking In Fear And Dread

Its Empty Comfort

Alcoholic Dreams

Depression Taking Its Toll

Shutters In The Night

Temptation Beckons

Life Bitter By Deadly Drinks

No Escape From Hell

Mind Lost In A Haze

Numbed By Addiction's Kiss

A Betrayed Lover

Searching For Normal

Desolate Longing Consumes

Never Fitting In

Cravings Drain My Strength

Trying To Flee Addiction

A New Life Awaits

Clouds Of Despair Part

Fading Away In God's Grace

Brave Journey Begins

Mettle And Courage

Paving Path Of Healing Hope

Building Inner Strength

Grim Shadows Fading

The Mind Becoming Clearer

Fighting Through Darkness

Newfound Blissfulness

Replacing Cravings With Joy

A Beacon Of Light

Painful Memories

Addiction's Hold Breaking

Embracing Freedom

Wounds Starting To Heal

Sobriety Gains Its Place

The World Comes Alive

Dawn Of A New Day

Strength Abounding Within Soul

Resilience Growing

Chained By Fear No More

Days Filled With Serenity

A Life Worth Living

The Journey Starting

Persistence And New Faith Shine

A Path To Freedom

Depression Fading

A New Dawn Bravely Awaits

A Clear Sober Mind

Love & Joy

Eyes Meet Across Room

Attraction Clear And Present

The Start Of Something

He Drops To One Knee

A Black Box With A Red Bow

The Start Of Their Life

Love Is What We Seek

Respect, Trust, Safety, Kindness

Keys To Lasting Love

Baby Draws First Breath

Cries Out Into Their New World

Beautiful Life Born

It Is Not Easy

Sometimes We Can Fall Apart

But Love Remains True

Unrequited Love

Longing Deep Within My Heart

A Sadness Inside

Love So Sweet, It Hums

Like A Summer Song Of Bliss

Melting Hearts That Kiss

Soft And Gentle Love

Wraps Around Like Summer Sun

In A Warm Embrace

The Sun Sparkles Bright

Sky Ablaze With Rainbow Light

True Love Never Fades

Shared Moments Linger

Filling Hearts With Gentle Joy

A Love So Divine

Laughter Fills The Air

Smiles Last For Eternity

Forever In Love

Simple Joy Of Life

A Remarkable Feeling

Love Overflowing

A Blissful Feeling
Joyful Laughter Fills The Air
Bright Smiling Faces

Children In The Park
Snippets Of Joyous Chit-Chat
Sharing In Delight

Rays Of Happiness

The Sunlight Shines So Brightly

Perfect Day To Live

Feeling Uplifted

Delicate Scent Of Flowers

Joy Is Everywhere

Warmth That Radiates

Filling Me With Blissful Glow

Spreading Peace Throughout

In Moments Of Ease

Calm And Content With Myself

I Found Joy To Keep

Sunrays On My Skin

Gentle Breeze Caressing Me

True Delight I Feel

Live In The Present

No Worries Of What Will Come

Sense Of Elation

Love of Family

Like A Dazzling Star That Shines

Joyous Bond Of Life

Precious Moments Shared

Cherished Memories That Last

A Timeless Treasure

As Time Passes By

Families Faithful And True

The Love Of Those Close

The Warmth Of Friendship

A True Joy That Knows No Bounds

Truest Companions

A Circle Of Friends

Sharing In Life's Adventures

Connections That Last

Each Smile And Laugh Shared

Memories Made Together

Bonds That Never Break

Friendship Is A Gift

Brings Us Closer When Apart

Are There When Needed

Gentle Purr Of Cats

Bringing Laughter And Comfort

Innate Joy They Bring

The Bark Of A Pup

Filling Ears With Cheerful Sound

Delightful Surprise

A Wag Of The Tail

An Unconditional Love

An Embrace Of Joy

Soft Furry Bodies

Warm Comfort Radiating

Caring Companions

The Joy Pets Bring Us

Far Beyond What We Expect

Brightening Our Days

Morning Sun Rises

A Newborn Baby Giggles

Tiny Hands Reach Out

Sweet Smell Of New Life

The Sight Of Those Tiny Feet

Bundle Of Delight

Small Dainty Fingers

Perfect, Soft And Delicate

Bringing Sense Of Peace

Staring In Wonder

Enchanted By The Small Things

A Wondrous New World

Such Much Tenderness

Divine Blessing From Above

A Loving Embrace

A Heartfelt Laughter

Ripples Of Pleasure Through Me

Heart Brimming With Joy

A Beautiful Day

Delightfully Fulfilled Mood

Lingers Within Me

Warmth Of Happiness

Radiates Out Like Sunshine

Brings Me Contentment

The Warmth Of My Love

My Beautiful Wife's Embrace

Timeless Devotion

In A Blissful State

Wrapped In Her Tender Caress

Divine Connection

Sparkle In Her Eyes

Her Gentle Touch And Warm Smile

Unconditional

My Love For Her Grows

Each Passing Moment We Share

The Ultimate Bond

Our Story Is Love

Leaving Us Both Feeling Blessed

Joy That Overflows

Loss & Death

Caught Up In Danger

Deciding On Fight Or Flight

Must Make Decision

Shots During The Night

Blood Lining The City Streets

Youth Paying The Price

Enters Bodega

He Quickly Withdraws His Gun

It Goes Bad, Clerk Dies

Convicted Felon

Serving Two Life Sentences

Murder In The First

Sharp Pain Shoots Down Arm

Chest Heavy, Dizzy, Sweating

The Reaper Watches

Blood Splatters The Wall

Powerless Over Life's Pain

Gun Falls To The Floor

Passing From This Life

Wondering What Lays Beyond

The Darkness Of Death

Strapped To The Table

Injections For The Guilty

The Debt Must Be Paid

Blade At The Ready

Hesitation Shows The Doubt

Having Second Thoughts

The Final Chapter

The Book Of Life Now Closing

What Did Your Life Add

Old, Tired, And Worn Out

Age Catches Us All In Time

Ready To Move On

Life Is Fleeting Here

This Spinning Wheel We Call Home

Death Will Come For Us

Despite The Darkness

Grateful For The Days Given

Knowing Death Will Come

Nature's Beauty Fades

As It Calls Us To Its Fold

No One Can Escape

As I Say Goodbye

The Time Stands Still In My Heart

Softly Parting Ways

The Sun Slowly Sets

Painful Memories Linger

Goodbye Is Too Hard

Thoughts Of You Haunt Me

Lingering Like A Bad Song

My Heart Says Goodbye

Emotions So Deep

An Ache That Won't Ever Ease

Your Absence Looms Large

Hushed Whisper Of Grief

Echoes Through The Night Darkness

Pain Of Loss Lingers

Sudden Loss Of Child

Her Silent Tears Will Not Dry

Lost Forevermore

The Memories Fade

Aching With Unspoken Words

Empty Embrace Felt

Gone Are Days Of Joy

Sun Never Shines Quite As Bright

Fades In Sorrow's Light

Pain Of Deep Sorrow

Heavy Heartaches Lingers

Endless Grief And Tears

Life Filled With Despair

Lonely Roads Of Grief And Pain

Numbness Overwhelms

Clouds Of Darkness Shade

Light Too Far To Reach From Here

Desolate Are Days

Failed Hopes And Lost Dreams

A Hollowed Out Shell Remains

Lost Soul Without Peace

No Jovial Smiles

Grief Is Ever Present Now

Healing Takes Its Time

Life Ends Abruptly

Nothing Can Stop The Darkness

The Pain Of Death Felt

No More Laughter Heard

An Empty Void Left Behind

Grief That Never Fades

A Light Extinguished

No More Life Or Joy In Sight

Tears Flow Endlessly

Hearts Broken And Torn

Pain Of Separation Deep

Loneliness Remains

Dreams Lost In Death's Wake

Farewells Said With Sorrow

Endless Mourning Cry

Embraces Silent

Mourning Souls Linger In Night

Death's Finality

Tears Of Sadness Flow

Hearts Shattered From The Goodbye

Loss That Never Fades

Sorrowful Moments

Resigned To Fate's Cold Desire

Fading Existence

Final Breaths Taken

No More Joy Or Peace In Sight

Only Loneliness

Memories Haunt Me

Absence Of A Loved One Here

Grief Beyond Compare

Waves Of Longing Come

Lost Ones Never To Be Seen

Sharing Bitter Tears

Coldness Now Pervades

Shadows That Cannot Be Seen

Peace Eludes Us All

Grief In Soft Whispers

Echoing Through The Night Sky

Pain Never Abates

Light Of Joy Dimming

Shadows Of Sorrow Creep In

Cries Endless Mourning

Joyous Days Are Gone

Not Even The Sun Can Warm

Hearts Remain So Cold

The Sweetest Goodbye

Desperate Final Embrace

A Void Left Behind

No Solace To Find

Lost Souls Wander Aimlessly

Grief Keeps Marching On

Darkness All Around

Hope Fades Into Dark Despair

Sorrow Too Heavy

Sun Is Setting Soon

A Cold Darkness Falls So Deep

The Sweet Call Beckons

Darkness Creeping In

Curling Like A Silent Fog

An Endless Bleak Night

A Deep Dark Sorrow

A Pain With No End In Sight

Lost In My Despair

Tears Of Loneliness

My Friends Are No Longer Here

Alone I Face This

Old And All Alone

No More Joy Or Laughter Here

Only Time Is Left

Trapped Deep In My Fear

Drowning In Sorrow And Hate

Engulfing Darkness

Everything Else

Happy But Still Sad

Stacy Rocking The Baby

Clean And Safe From Jake

Stacy Moving On

Her Parents Show Their Support

Rebuilding Her Life

Out In The Blackness

Two Hundred And Fifty Miles

The Station Orbits

Yorktown's Battle Field

Where Bloodiest Battle Fought

Ending Of The War

Destroying The Chains

Abraham Lincoln Stood Tall

Remembered Always

Martin Luther King

Dreaming Of Equality

Civil Rights Leader

Rosa Parks Was Strong

Her Stand Brought About A Change

Hope For Equal Life

White House In DC

Symbol Our Democracy

Standing Proud And Strong

Paul William Jurgens

Men Of Courage, Strength, And Hope

Thomas Mingione

The Bright Neon Signs

Synth-Pop Beats On Radio

The Nineteen Eighties

Back To The Future

Pac-Man And The Rubik's Cube

Material Girl

An Era Of Change

Nirvana Rocked The Nation

Aaliyah Sings Soft

Power To Move Us

To Take Us Away From Here

Movie Memories

Dialing Symbols

Ancient Civilizations

Worlds Beyond Our Own

Whirlwind Energies

Gateway To Host Of Planets

Into Distant Worlds

The Force Live Within

Galaxies Far, Far Away

Darkness And Light Clash,

Lightsabers Glow Bright

Skywalker Versus Vader

A Legend Is Born

Wash At The Controls

Brave Captain Mal Reynolds Leads

Simon The Doctor

Shepherd's Cryptic Past

The Companion Inara

River Not All There

Zoe's The Loyal One

Jayne Is The Stubborn Hired Gun

Kaylee Mechanic

Alliance Control

Fighting For Freedom Their Way

Outlaws In The Stars

Cylon War Rages

Battlestar Galactica

Save Humanity

Vipers Soar Through Space

Colonial Flag Displayed

Looking For A Home

Search For Earth Begins

Their Hope Carries Them Forward

Dangers Lay Ahead

Traveling Doctor

Always Racing Through Space-Time

Exploring The Realms

Adventures Abound

Solving Mysteries Galore

Brave Heart Never Stops

The Faithful TARDIS

Transporting Trusty Blue Box

Going Somewhere New

The Daleks Hate Him

Cybermen Seek To Control

His Wits Set Him Free

Mulder And Scully

Uncovering Dark Secrets

In Search Of The Truth

Cryptids From The Wild

UFOs In The Night Sky

Conspiracy Looms

Suspenseful Missions

Aliens From Other Realms

Danger Closes Fast

Saved Within Their Stack

Rebirth Of The Human Soul

A Future Unknown

Sleeved Human Puppets

Minds Transferred To New Body

Mortality Gone

The Darkness Of Space

Babylon 5 Shines With Light,

Protect From The Night

Strange Creatures Onboard

Interspersed Among Humans

From Distant Places

Vorlons And Shadows

Pit Brother Against Brother

War Of Cosmic Scale

Traveling In Time

Sam Beckett On A Mission

Make Things Right Again

Punk Rockers Rage On

Rebelling Conformity

Youthful Energy

Mosh Pits And Long Hair

Loud Riffs And Screaming Vocals

Noise Of Rebellion

A Social Movement

Breaking Rules, Rejecting Norms

Act Of Defiance

Bright Colors And Spikes

Safety Pins, Leather Jackets

The Look of Punk Rock

Three chord progressions

Music Of Revolution

Anthems For The Young

The King Of Horror

Macabre Tales Of Terror

Horrors That Haunt Us

Edgar Allan Poe

Raven Caws In Midnight's Gloom

Mysteries Sublime

Perplexing Poet

Penning Works Of Frightful Lore

Words Of Death And Doom

Creative Genius

Gripping Masterpieces Born

Legend John Steinbeck

Engaging Readers

Classics Of Realism Craft

Beauty In His Words

Steinbeck's Mastery

Realism Literature

Dialogue Rings True

Cowering In Fear

Propaganda Fills Airwaves

Government Control

A Lonely Warren

Their Home And Life In Danger

Rabbits On The Rise

Epic Quest, Brave Hearts

Friendship Binds Them Together

Fate of Middle Earth.

Traveling Through Lands

An Unlikely Fellowship

In Dark Times Set Forth

Battling Orcs And Men

Strength In The Meekest of Souls

Hope Light The Darkness

Ring Of Power Found

The Shire Must Be Defended

Search Of Mount Doom's Flame

Enduring Each Day

Using Science And His Grit

Trying To Survive

Berlin Wall Falls Down

Iron Curtain Ripped Apart

A New Era Dawns

11/14/11

www.ingramcontent.com/pod-product-compliance
Lightning Source LLC
Chambersburg PA
CBHW030144200626
46812CB00015B/1416